THIS WALKER BOOK BELONGS TO:

Don't Let the Pigeon Stay Up Late!

words and pictures by mo willems

For Trixie at bedtime

WALKER BOOKS
AND SUBSIDIARIES
LONDON · BOSTON · SYDNEY · AUCKLAND

First published in Great Britain 2007 by
Walker Books Ltd, 87 Vauxhall Walk, London SE11 5HJ

10 9 8 7

© 2006 Mo Willems

The moral rights of the author have been asserted

First published in the United States by Hyperion Books for Children.
British publication rights arranged with Sheldon Fogelman Agency, Inc.

This book has been handlettered by Mo Willems

Printed in Singapore

British Library Cataloguing in Publication Data:
a catalogue record for this book is available from
the British Library

ISBN 978-1-4063-0812-9

www.walker.co.uk

Can I have a glass of water?

Studies show that pigeons hardly nee any sleep at all!

It's the middle of the day in Alaska!

I'll go to bed early tomorrow night instead!

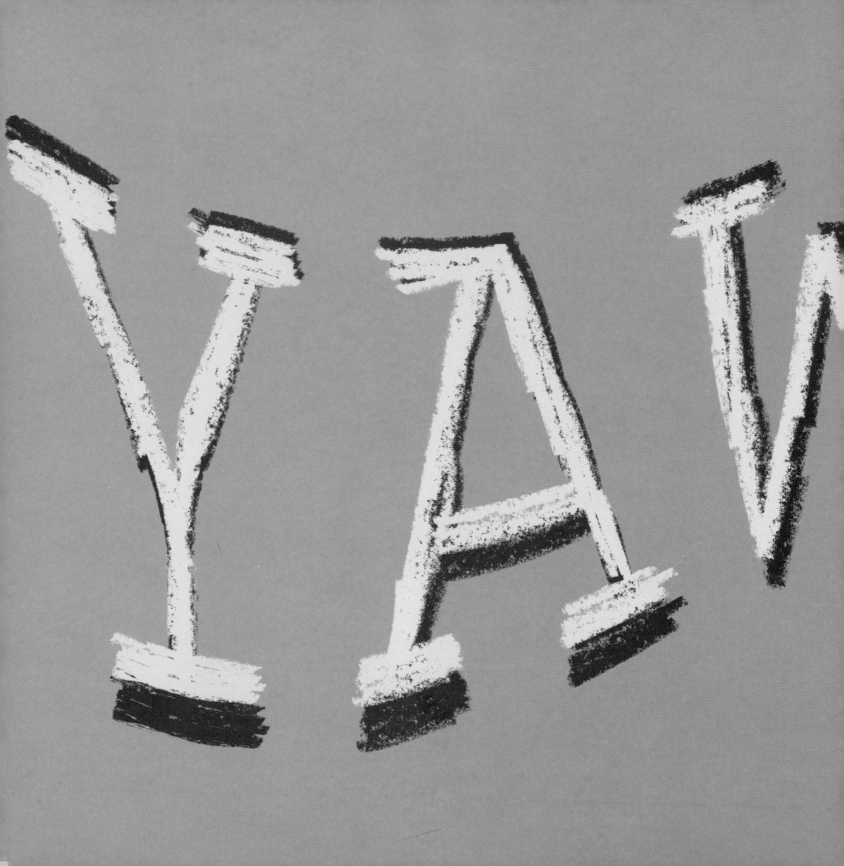

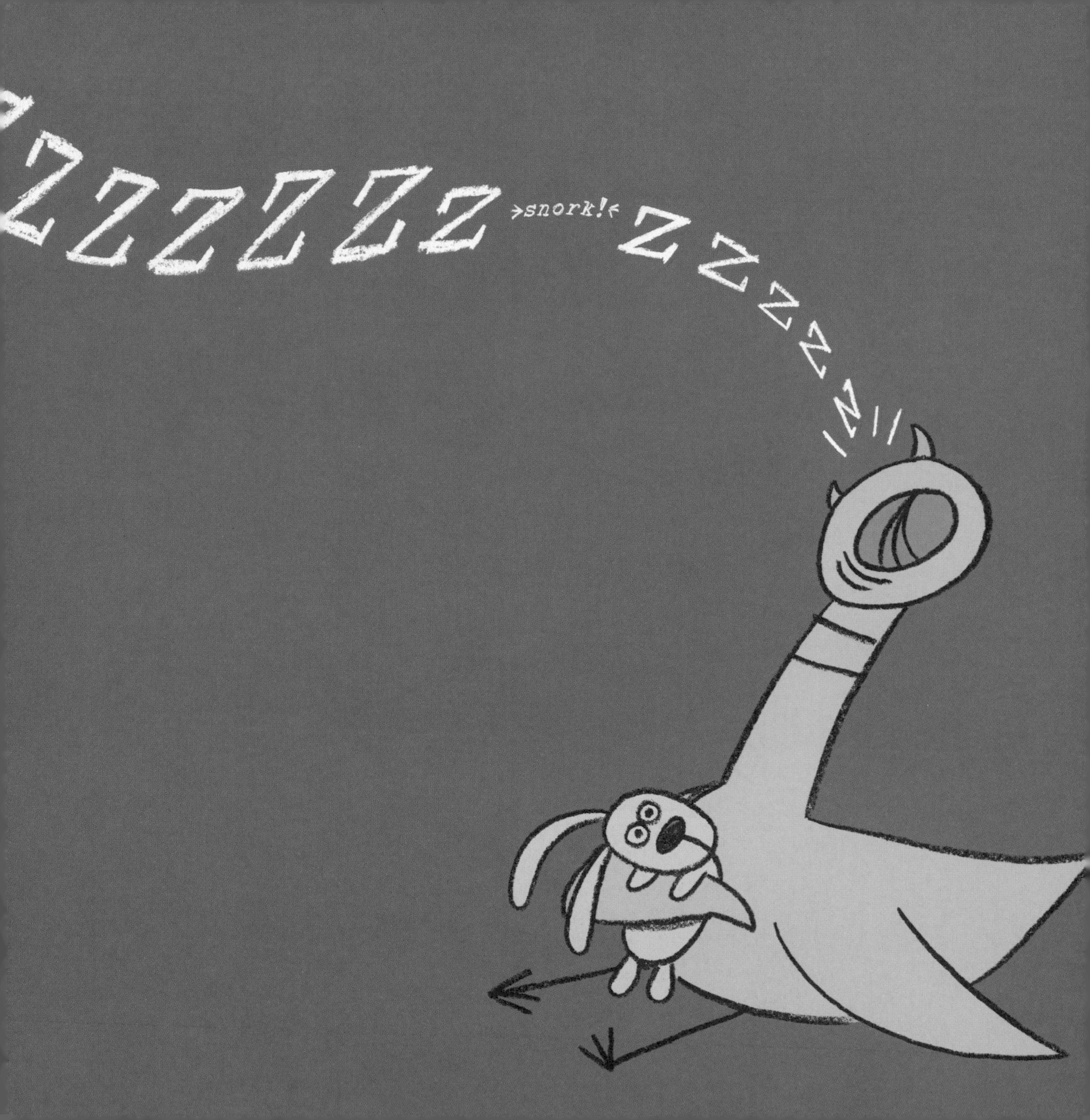
ZZZZZZz
→snork!←
ZZZZZZ

WALKER BOOKS is the world's leading
independent publisher of children's books.
Working with the best authors and illustrators
we create books for all ages, from babies
to teenagers – books your child will
grow up with and always remember. So…

FOR THE BEST CHILDREN'S BOOKS,
LOOK FOR THE BEAR